For Kit and Arthur, who saw the seal
and heard the music, and for the children
of Harold Magnay School, Liverpool,
for their inspiration

MICHAEL FOREMAN

SEAL SURFER

HARCOURT BRACE & COMPANY

San Diego   New York   London

Printed in Italy

SPRING

ONE DAY in early spring an old man and his grandson, Ben, carefully climbed down to a rocky beach. They were looking for mussels.

As Ben searched he noticed a slight movement among the rocks. Then he saw the seal. It was difficult to see her body against the rocks, except for a smudge of red on her belly.

"Look, Granddad!" Ben cried. "The seal is injured."

"Don't get too close," warned Granddad. They watched the seal from a distance.

The seal looked quite calm, lying still in the morning sun, and after a while Ben started hunting for mussels again.

When he next looked up at the seal, he saw a flash of white. A newly born seal pup nuzzled her mother.

"Quick, Granddad," whispered Ben. "Let's get some fish for the seals."

❧

As the spring days lengthened, Ben and his granddad often watched the seal family from the cliff top. The pup's white coat molted and she became the color of the rocks. Sometimes she moved to the water's edge to watch her mother fish. As she basked in the warm sun, she kept an eye on Ben and his granddad.

SUMMER

IN EARLY SUMMER Ben watched as the mother seal pushed her pup off the rocks and into the sea. The shock of the cold water made the young seal panic. The water closed over her head. She pushed upward with her tail and flippers until her head burst through the surface.

Her mother plunged into the water, and together they swam around and around—diving, twisting, corkscrewing into the depths. When the seal pup broke through the water's surface, she heard the boy cheer.

AUTUMN

THE SUMMER DAYS faded. One evening Ben went down to the harbor to meet his granddad, who was returning from a day's fishing. Granddad's old pickup truck sat with the door open and the radio on. The music of Beethoven filled the air.

Granddad stared into the water. A whiskery face stared back at him like a reflection in the moonlit mirror of the harbor.

Granddad tossed the seal a fish—and then another. Ben watched as the mirror dissolved, reformed, and then dissolved again as they all shared the music of Beethoven.

WINTER

WHILE THE WET winter winds buffeted the boy on his way to school, the young seal learned the lessons of the sea.

The seal loved to swim far from home, exploring the coast. She learned to fish by swimming deep and looking up to see the fish outlined against the sky.

She slept at sea, floating upright like a bottle, with just her nose above the surface. Best of all she loved to haul herself up onto the rocks with other young seals to feel the sun and wind on her skin.

But one day the wind rose suddenly into a full-blown gale. Rain and mountainous waves wrenched great rocks from the cliffs. The young seals dived deep, trying to escape falling boulders. But even in the sea they were in danger. Some seals were dashed against the rocks by the waves.

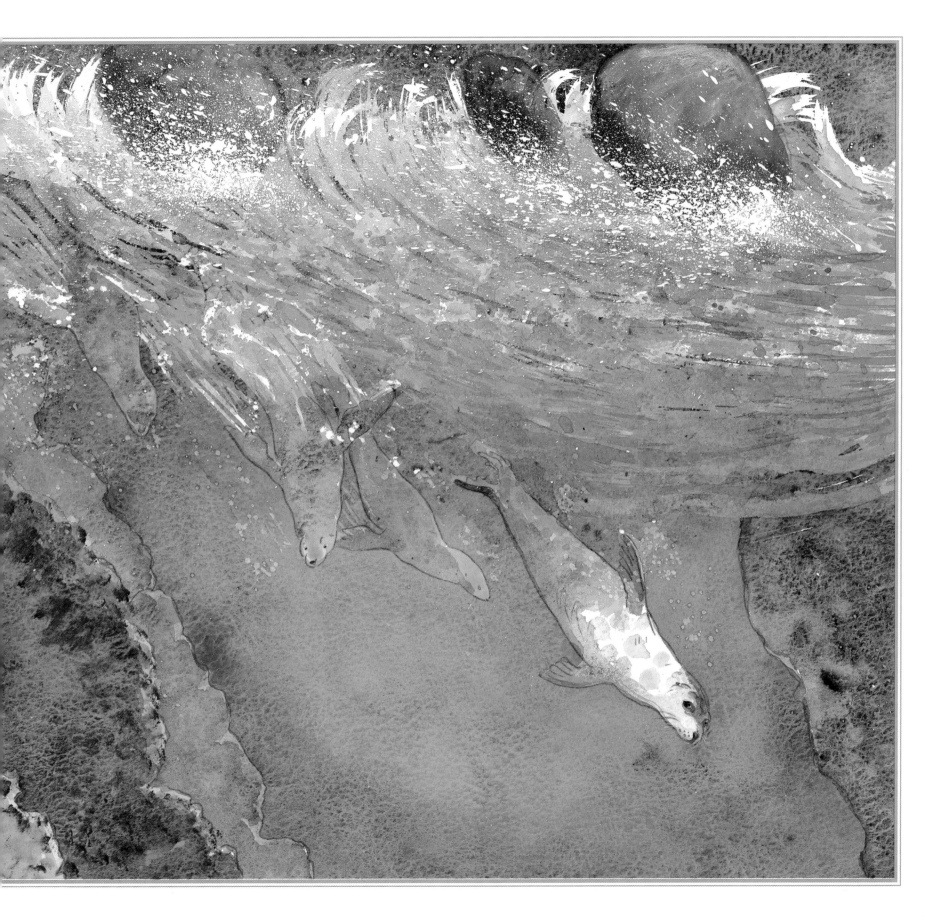

SPRING

THE WARMTH OF SPRING brought wildflowers and Ben and his granddad to the cliffs once more. But there was no sign of the young seal.

"She must have died in the winter storms," said Ben.

But sometimes the mother seal still came to the harbor for an evening of fish and music.

SUMMER

As SPRING WARMED into summer, Ben went every Saturday to Surf School. He was a strong swimmer, and after much practice he and the other new surfers were ready to catch some waves.

One sunny day Ben lay on his board as it rose and fell on the gently rocking swell. Suddenly he was aware of a quick movement in the water. A dark shape swooped under the board. The gleaming face of the young seal popped up beside his own. Ben was elated. "You're alive!" he called, grinning.

The sea gathered itself for some big waves. The dark green walls of water lined up along the horizon. The seal sensed the movement of the water. Ben and the seal let the first two waves pass, then together they rode the third huge, rolling wave toward the shore.

All afternoon Ben and the seal surfed together. Then just as quickly as she had appeared, the seal was gone. Ben waited awhile and then let the next good wave carry him to the sand.

The next day the tide was perfect and the young seal was back. Again Ben and the seal surfed side by side.

Ben could not take his eyes off the seal as she flashed through the water. As he concentrated on watching her, the wave he was riding suddenly broke and plunged him headfirst off his board. He somersaulted through the surf and struck a rock. The water, thick with sand, filled his nose and mouth. His body was pulled deeper and deeper. He was sinking into darkness.

Then he felt a different sensation. His body was forced upward. Sunlight shone through the water onto Ben's face as the seal pushed his body up. With a final heave she flipped Ben onto his board. He held on, and the next wave carried him to the shore. His friends crowded around to make sure he was all right. Once he caught his breath, Ben felt fine.

The next afternoon, and for the rest of the long, hot summer, Ben surfed with the seal.

WINTER

THE WONDERFUL SUMMER and gentle autumn were followed by the worst of winters. The storms smacked the rocks and churned up the sand and stones. The beach was deserted. No seals came there.

And maybe one day he would lie on the cliff tops with his own grandchildren and together they would watch the seals.

☙

First U.S. edition 1997
First published in Great Britain in 1996 by Andersen Press Ltd.

Library of Congress Cataloging-in-Publication Data
Foreman, Michael.
Seal surfer/[author and illustrator] Michael Foreman.
p.   cm.
Summary: Although he is on crutches, a boy goes to the beach with his grandfather,
where they watch a seal being born, and over the following seasons, the boy and the seal develop a special bond.
ISBN 0-15-201399-7
[1. Physically handicapped—Fiction. 2. Seals (Animals)—Fiction.] I. Title.
PZ7.F75829Se   1997
[Fic]—dc20   96-1182

A C E F D B

Printed in Italy